It's Christmas!

**But Dad's lost his job so we have to think
of ways to make some money.**

**Looks like my brother's famous bottom
might come to the rescue again . . .**

C153962272

Jeremy Strong once worked in a bakery, putting the jam into three thousand doughnuts every night. Now he puts the jam in stories instead, which he finds much more exciting. At the age of three, he fell out of a first-floor bedroom window and landed on his head. His mother says that this damaged him for the rest of his life and refuses to take any responsibility. He loves writing stories because he says it is 'the only time you alone have complete control and can make anything happen'. His ambition is to make you laugh (or at least snuffle). Jeremy Strong lives near Bath with his wife, Gillie, four cats and a flying cow.

Are you feeling silly enough to read more?

BATPANTS!
THE BATTLE FOR CHRISTMAS (A Cosmic Pyjamas Adventure)
THE BEAK SPEAKS
BEWARE! KILLER TOMATOES
CHICKEN SCHOOL
CHRISTMAS CHAOS FOR THE HUNDRED-MILE-AN-HOUR DOG
DINOSAUR POX
DOCTOR BONKERS! (A Cosmic Pyjamas Adventure)
GIANT JIM AND THE HURRICANE
THE HUNDRED-MILE-AN-HOUR DOG
KRANKENSTEIN'S CRAZY HOUSE OF HORROR
(A Cosmic Pyjamas Adventure)
KRAZY COW SAVES THE WORLD – WELL, ALMOST
LOST! THE HUNDRED-MILE-AN-HOUR DOG
MY BROTHER'S FAMOUS BOTTOM
THERE'S A PHARAOH IN OUR BATH!
THERE'S A VIKING IN MY BED AND OTHER STORIES

JEREMY STRONG'S LAUGH-YOUR-SOCKS-OFF JOKE BOOK
JEREMY STRONG'S LAUGH-YOUR-SOCKS-OFF EVEN
MORE JOKE BOOK

LAUGH YOUR SOCKS OFF WITH Jeremy STRONG

My Brother's Christmas Bottom - Unwrapped!

Illustrated by Rowan Clifford

PUFFIN

PUFFIN BOOKS

Published by the Penguin Group
Penguin Books Ltd, 80 Strand, London WC2R 0RL, England
Penguin Group (USA) Inc., 375 Hudson Street, New York, New York 10014, USA
Penguin Group (Canada), 90 Eglinton Avenue East, Suite 700, Toronto, Ontario, Canada M4P 2Y3
(a division of Pearson Penguin Canada Inc.)
Penguin Ireland, 25 St Stephen's Green, Dublin 2, Ireland (a division of Penguin Books Ltd)
Penguin Group (Australia), 250 Camberwell Road, Camberwell, Victoria 3124, Australia
(a division of Pearson Australia Group Pty Ltd)
Penguin Books India Pvt Ltd, 11 Community Centre, Panchsheel Park, New Delhi – 110 017, India
Penguin Group (NZ), 67 Apollo Drive, Rosedale, North Shore 0632, New Zealand
(a division of Pearson New Zealand Ltd)
Penguin Books (South Africa) (Pty) Ltd, 24 Sturdee Avenue, Rosebank, Johannesburg 2196, South Africa

Penguin Books Ltd, Registered Offices: 80 Strand, London WC2R 0RL, England

puffinbooks.com

First published 2010
1

Text copyright © Jeremy Strong, 2010
Illustrations copyright © Rowan Clifford, 2009, 2010
Extract copyright © Jeremy Strong, 2009
All rights reserved

The moral right of the author and illustrator has been asserted

Set in Baskerville
Made and printed in Great Britain by Clays Ltd, St Ives plc

Except in the United States of America, this book is sold subject to the condition that it shall not, by way of
trade or otherwise, be lent, re-sold, hired out, or otherwise circulated without the publisher's prior consent
in any form of binding or cover other than that in which it is published and without a similar condition
including this condition being imposed on the subsequent purchaser

British Library Cataloguing in Publication Data
A CIP catalogue record for this book is available from the British Library

ISBN: 978-0-141-32808-9

www.greenpenguin.co.uk

Penguin Books is committed to a sustainable future
for our business, our readers and our planet.
The book in your hands is made from paper
certified by the Forest Stewardship Council.

This is for my grandchildren, Sam and Ben.

Please keep your bottoms well wrapped.

I hope this story makes you laugh.

KENT LIBRARIES & ARCHIVES	
C153962272	

Contents

1. Doom and Gloom for Christmas   1

2. What a Lovely Clean Car You   12
   Have, Mr Tugg!

3. Who's the Poop-a-doodle Noodle-brain?   25

4. Here Come the Christmas Vampires   39

5. A Weapon of Mass Destruction   49

6. Some Unwrapped Cheese   64

7. It's Raining Indoors!   71

8. I'm in Heaven   85

9. A Bit of Zap!   97

10. Mr Tugg Gets RUDE!   111

1 Doom and Gloom for Christmas

BIG PROBLEMO! Dad's lost his job. He's been working at the paper factory for YEARS AND YEARS. Now it's going to close down. Dad's fed up and not like his usual cheery self at all. He hardly speaks to anyone and when he does he says very gloomy things.

'It's almost Christmas and there won't be any money for food or presents or jolly holly stuff like a Christmas tree. No balloons, no Christmas cake –'

'Hooray!' I shouted. 'No Christmas cake! I HATE Christmas cake. It tastes like YUCK. In fact it tastes like yuck with muck.'

Mum was upset. 'Nicholas, if you don't mind, I go to a lot of trouble to make our Christmas cake each year and most people love it.'

'I don't,' I reminded her.

'It's YUCK!' laughed Cheese. 'Nicky said it's yuck.' He stuck out his tongue and made revolting noises. Cheese is my little bother, I mean *brother*. I've also got a little pester, I mean *sister*. She's called Tomato. Cheese and Tomato are twins.

Odd names, aren't they? That's because they were born in the back of a pizza delivery van and Dad said they ought to be called Cheese and Tomato. The names stuck. My dad's always thinking up silly things. At least he was before he lost his job.

Anyhow, Mum wasn't going to give up. 'Some people,' she went on, 'LOVE my Christmas cake. So there.'

None of this cheered up Dad. 'There's no

point in making one this year,' he muttered. 'We'll have to cancel Christmas.'

'It'll be all right,' Mum said. 'No need to panic. We can get by. We'll just have to cut back a bit.'

Our house was getting more dismal by the second! Tomato stuck out her lower lip and did her best to look like a picnic in a downpour.

Cheese threw himself across Mum's lap and wailed, 'I WANT CHRISTMAS!'

'There are still five weeks to go before Christmas,' Mum said evenly. 'I'm sure by that time everything will be all right.'

Cheese sniffed loudly and looked at Dad to see if he agreed but Dad was standing at the window, staring gloomily out at the rain.

BOY OH BOY! Were we getting miserable, or what? Maybe I could do something to help. I thought hard. Aha! 'I could get some work,' I suggested. 'I could do a paper round or something like that.'

At least it put a smile on Mum's face. 'That's a

kind idea, Nicholas, but I'm sure we can get by. I have my part-time job at the school, so that's one good thing, and maybe we can make our Christmas presents this year instead of buying them.'

Cheese stared at Mum, aghast, and collapsed on the floor in a crushed heap. 'You can't make a space ship!' he sobbed.

'Of course we can,' Mum said cheerfully. 'We can get some old yoghurt pots and used toilet

rolls and some tin foil and you can use your felt tips and . . .'

'NOT A SILLY TOILET POTTY SPACE SHIP!' yelled Cheese. 'A, A, A REAL SPACE SHIP THAT REALLY GOES INTO REAL SPACE!' He gave an almighty sniff and hurried on. 'And I'm on board and so are Rubbish and, and, and Captain Birdseye and Poop, Beaky and Leaky and Mavis Moppet and ALL the rabbits.'

By this time we were all staring at Cheese in

amazement. He wanted to take all the backyard animals into space! Even Dad came out of his World of Gloom.

'Jumping jellyfish! You can't put our goat and all our chickens and rabbits into a space ship. It would be like Noah's Ark – and the messiest, smelliest space ship ever.'

Tomato looked across at her twin brother and shrugged. 'Anyway,' she began, very matter-of-factly. 'You can't go into space because you won't be able to breathe and if you don't breathe you DIE, don't you, Daddy?'

'Um, yes, that is true,' Dad admitted. 'Unless you have a space suit. It's always a good idea to wear a space suit if you're going into space.'

Cheese frowned hard for a moment and then suddenly hit on the answer. 'That's my second present I want – a space suit.'

Dad raised his eyebrows at Mum. 'Don't think you can make a space suit out of yoghurt pots and toilet rolls,' he said, getting gloomy again.

6

'Well . . .' Mum started.

'Aha!' cried Dad, interrupting, and the gloom vanished. 'I've got an idea.' He waggled a finger in the air for a moment and then stopped. 'Hmm. No I haven't. It won't work.'

'What was it?' asked Mum.

'I told you, it won't work,' Dad insisted.

'Tell us!' snapped Mum.

'OK. We get a bath and we put it outside the shopping centre in the middle of town. We fill the bath with something daft – baked beans, tinned tomatoes, marmalade, sausages, cold chips –'

'All right,' said Mum. 'We get the idea. Then what?'

'Well, there'll be loads of people watching us by then, so I say: "I bet you one pound that my wife will lie down in that bath." And they say: "Of course she won't. You're on." And then you get in the bath and lie down and we get a pound from everyone!'

Mum folded her arms. 'I'm not getting into a

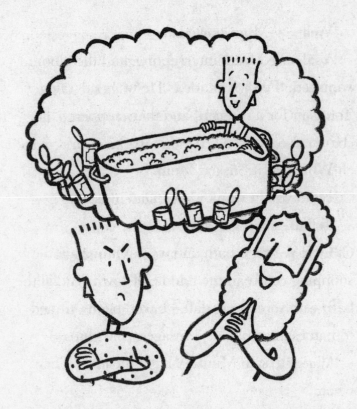

stinky old bath full of splodge,' she said.

Dad sighed. 'That's why it won't work. I told you it wouldn't. Then I realized that we haven't got a spare bath to get into and that's another reason why it won't work.'

Silence fell. Tomato's bottom lip started to quiver again.

'Maybe we could sell something?' I suggested.

Dad's face exploded into a huge smile. 'Of course! Sell something! We'll sell Cheese and Tomato! They could be used as ornaments. They could sit at either end of a mantelpiece and make cheerful chirpy noises!'

Dad flopped his hands like little paws. '*Wheep, wheep, wheep!*' he squeaked in a tiny voice. 'I'm a Christmas Elf, and I'm sitting on your shelf!'

'You're a Christmas Turkey, more like,' Mum laughed. 'And you know we can't sell the twins.'

'OK, how about we sell our car?' Dad said.

'I need it,' Mum replied flatly.

'How about we sell Mr Tugg's car?' Dad suggested.

Mum smiled. 'He's our next-door neighbour, you daft bumblebrain! He'd probably explode.'

Mum was certainly right there. Mr Tugg is famous for exploding. He's really good at it. In fact he'd make a brilliant firework. This is what he'd be like:

1. Light the blue touch paper and stand well clear!
2. Smoke pours out of Mr Tugg's ears.
3. Sparks shoot out of his eyes.
4. *BOOM! BANG!* Aerial bombs whizz from his mouth and explode all around.
5. His arms and legs whirl round like Catherine wheels.
6. And finally – his head explodes and falls off!

Anyhow, all that talk of cars had given me a better idea. 'Why don't we set up our own car wash?' I suggested. 'We could stand out on the street with a sign that says CAR WASH. All we need is a bucket of soapy water and some sponges and cloths.'

Mum relaxed back into her armchair. 'Thank

heavens there are at least two sensible people in this family,' she declared.

'Two? Who are they?' asked Dad, puzzled, looking at Cheese and Tomato and shrugging his shoulders.

'Me and Nicholas,' Mum answered sharply. 'You were born daft and you'll stay daft.'

'Thank you very much,' said Dad happily. 'Right then, I shall just go and have a bath. Where are the baked beans?'

'Daddy's going to have a bean bath!' shouted Cheese.

'Silly Daddy!' added Tomato.

Mum laughed. 'And I'm going to get the bucket and sponges,' she said. 'Car washing, here we come.'

2. What a Lovely Clean Car You Have, Mr Tugg!

```
CAR WASHING.
GIVE YOUR CAR A CHRISTMAS
CLEAN-UP!
SOAPY WASH AND RINSE – £5.00
SOAPY WASH, RINSE AND DRY – £7.50
```

That's what our sign said, and guess who the first customer was? Only my headteacher, Mrs Underdone!

I have noticed something odd about cars and their drivers. Quite often you see a huge car – maybe one of those ground-crunching four-wheel-drive monsters – and it comes to a halt.

Then the driver gets out and they're like some teeny-tiny ant person.

And then you see a tiny car – maybe it's one of those weeny-meeny tinny-Mini things that could probably drive down a rabbit hole. It comes to a halt and the driver gets out and they are mega-gigantic, like an elephant. (Tomato calls them bellypants!)

Well, Mrs Underdone has a four-wheel-drive tank and she is an ant person. She is very slim too

and could probably climb through the letterbox
on your front door. She has a quiet, soft voice
that sounds like milk chocolate.

'Oooh, what a LAAARRVELEE idea,'
chortled Mrs Underdone, jumping down from
the car. 'I definitely need some Christmas sparkle.
I'll have the full works – soapy wash, rinse and
dry.'

'And what about the car?' winked Dad.

My face went bright red with embarrassment!

For two seconds Mrs Underdone looked rather
puzzled. Then she beamed a wicked smile at my
dad. 'Oh, you are daft!' she cried, giving Dad a
playful poke. 'I mean the car, of course.'

Dad silently mouthed the words 'Me? Daft?' at
me and tried to look hurt, but I knew he was only
play-acting, as usual. Anyway, I love him being
crazy! I'd hate to have a serious or boring dad.

We got Mrs Underdone's car all clean and
shiny. She was very pleased and we'd made our
first bit of money.

Then who should coming roaring round the
corner but Granny and Lancelot with their
mega-motorbike and sidecar. Granny was driving
and she almost did a hand-brake turn, except
that she didn't have a hand-brake.

Lancelot leaped out of the sidecar, pulling off
his helmet. 'Wow! That was some full stop we
came to there, honey-babe!' he laughed.

Honey-babe? How could he possibly call my gran
honey-babe? I mean to say, she's almost seventy!

'Do you wash motorbikes?' Lancelot asked. 'Is it cheaper? It should be, because they're smaller.'

Dad stroked his beard and eyed the chunky machine. 'We'll do the bike for four pounds, but the old lady will take a lot more scrubbing up so she'll be very expensive.'

That made Lancelot crease up with laughter. Granny didn't seem to think it was so funny.

'I heard that, Ronald. How dare you speak about your own mother like that? I've a good mind to send you to your room without any supper.'

'Mother, I'm forty-nine years old. Besides we don't live in the same house any longer.'

'Jolly good thing too, if you ask me,' muttered Granny. 'Are you going to wash this motorbike or not?'

Dad and I grabbed our buckets and made a pretty good job of it. Lancelot was so impressed he decided to tell his son. Now then, guess who Lancelot's son is? Mr Tugg – the human firework

who lives next door to us!

You'd never think they came from the same family. I mean, Lancelot is big and big-hearted, while Mr Tugg is short and short-tempered. Lancelot has his grey hair swept back in a ponytail. Mr Tugg is bald! They're complete opposites.

Mr Tugg came outside to inspect the car-washing team. He didn't seem all that happy but then he saw how sparkly his father's motorbike was.

 'I'll bring my car out of the garage and leave it on my drive. You can wash that too,' he said.

Dad tugged at the front of his hair and nodded. 'Arrr, thank 'ee kindly, sir,' he began in a silly voice. 'That be most kindly of 'ee.'

Mr Tugg's eyes narrowed. 'There's no need to be silly. Normally I wouldn't let you near my car. I haven't forgotten the time you allowed your pet alligator to sit in the back of it. However, I heard you lost your job and that can't be good just before Christmas. I'm only doing this to help you out,' he sniffed.

'Arrr, you be a right gentleman,' Dad drawled. 'I could tell you was a gentleman the moment I saw your shiny bald head, sir. I said to myself, I said: "Now Ron, that's either a gentleman coming along or a satellite dish with legs on it." An' lo and behold, it *were* a satellite dish on legs. An' now we're going to make your car even more sparkly than your head, sir.'

Mr Tugg let out a long-suffering sigh. 'I shall ignore your gibberish. Just get on and wash the car. I'll be back out in ten minutes to see how you're doing.'

Granny and Lancelot took off on their clean-gleam machine while Mr Tugg brought his car out from the garage, parked it on the drive and then disappeared indoors.

'We'd better make a good job of this,' I said to Dad.

'It's going to be the cleanest car in the country,' declared Dad. 'Let's get to work, Team Super-Wash! Give me five!' We did a high five. It would have worked a lot better if we hadn't BOTH been holding wet sponges. As they squidged together water sprayed out in every direction.

'Dad! I'm soaked!'

Do you know what Dad did? He began crooning to the tune of 'Singin' in the Rain'! *'We're sponging on the drive, We're sponging on the drive.*

What a glorious feeling, I'm glad to be alive!'

He stopped suddenly and dumped his bucket by Mr Tugg's front porch. 'Hey, Nick! I've just had a great idea. We could do this much more quickly with our garden hose. We can stretch it from our house – no problem.'

'Are you sure it will work?' I asked.

'Of course. It's perfect – and it'll be so much faster. We'll get this done in no time.'

Moments later Dad had unwound the hose and was spraying the car all over while I dashed about trying not to get soaked. It was certainly quicker – and also wetter. Dad danced round the car along with his song.

'I'm watering the car, it's better by far. It's such a good idea – I am such a star!'

That was when Mr Tugg came back out and he didn't seem very happy. In fact he had gone straight into a major firework explosion, fizzing and crackling all over the place.

'Turn off that hose! Can't you see the car's

front windows are open? Didn't you check? What kind of nitwit are you?'

'What? Can't hear you,' Dad shouted back, waving the hose all over the place so water sprayed in every direction. Mr Tugg ducked to avoid a soaking and came charging straight down the porch steps.

Unfortunately he didn't notice Dad's bucket and his left foot rammed straight into it.

'Aargh! What idiot put that bucket there? My foot's stuck and it's soaked through! Shut those car windows, you fool!'

Mr Tugg tried to reach Dad but the bucket on his foot slowed him down a lot. He looked like some mad escaped robot. And then he stumbled on the hose line. Mr Tugg didn't fall but he yanked on the hose and that made Dad swing round to see what was going on and he sprayed Mr Tugg with water, full frontal.

You'd think a wet firework wouldn't work, but this firework just got even more explosive!

'YOU BLITHERING BONE-BRAINED
BODGER! Turn off that hose! Look! Look what
you've done!'

I ran to our house and turned off the water
while Dad gazed sadly at our dripping neighbour.
'Oh dear,' he said. 'You are a bit wet, aren't you?'

'IT'S NOT ME – IT'S THE CAR!' yelled Mr

Tugg. 'LOOK AT IT! IT'S SOAKING!'

Dad was puzzled. 'You can't wash a car without it getting wet,' he pointed out.

'YOU DON'T WASH CARS ON THE INSIDE! THE WINDOWS WERE OPEN. LOOK WHAT YOU'VE DONE!'

Mr Tugg yanked open the driver's door and a

small lake gushed out, straight over both his feet. Then, complete with bucket-foot, he began to stagger towards Dad in a kind of squelchy lurch, arms and hands outstretched. I think he wanted to strangle him!

Dad opened his mouth to speak, then shut it again. He slowly turned to me, eyes wide with horror. 'Leg it!'

3. Who's the Poop-a-doodle Noodle-brain?

Guess what? We're not washing cars any longer. We've been banned by Mum. Anyhow, she reckons she's had a better idea.

'We are going to make things,' she announced.

'You've already suggested that, Mum,' I pointed out. 'Cheese went into terminal meltdown because he didn't want a space ship made from yoghurt pots.'

'That's not what I meant,' Mum said. 'We are going to make biscuits and cakes and gingerbread men. We'll dip some in chocolate. We'll tie ribbons on some so they can hang on the Christmas tree and we shall sell them.'

Tomato clapped her little hands. 'We're going to have a party!' she bubbled.

'It's not a party and the biscuits aren't for us,'
I tried to explain. 'We're going to sell them.'

'But I want some.' Tomato's lower lip began to
tremble. Tears were on their way.

'Me too!' cried Cheese. By this time Tomato
was clinging to my left leg and Cheese was
clinging to my right. The twins were ganging up
on me. Help!

'We want bickies!' they shouted.

I looked desperately at Mum. She laughed and came to the rescue.

'You can have some of the leftovers,' she told the twins and they let me go. Phew!

'And you can have some too, Nicholas.' Mum patted my head as if I was only four. Huh.

Dad wanted to know how we would sell the cakes and biscuits.

'I'm glad you asked,' said Mum, 'because I've had an idea for that too.'

'You're full of ideas today, aren't you?' grunted Dad. I think he was a bit annoyed actually. It's usually Dad who comes up with the bright ideas.

'Yes I am,' Mum said brightly. 'The thing is, we can make all sorts of different things for Christmas – tree decorations, mince pies, biscuits – anything we can think of. Then we sell everything at our Open Day.'

'Open Day?' Dad repeated suspiciously. 'What's our Open Day?'

'We open our house and garden to the public,' Mum said.

For several seconds there was a stunned silence. Then everyone began talking at once.

'We can't have people tramping all over the house!' cried Dad. 'This isn't a stately home, you know.'

'They can't come in my bedroom!' I added.

'Are we supposed to show them EVERYTHING?' shouted Dad, waving his arms around. 'Do we give them a guided tour and say "And here, Madam, is our lovely toilet? Take a look at our bath – do get in and try it out for yourself? Here, let me scrub your back?"'

'STOP BEING RIDICULOUS!' cried Mum. 'Of course it won't be like that. They will come into the downstairs only. We sell our bits and pieces and we serve them tea and coffee and cakes and so on. Also, they can see all the animals in our garden. It's like a mini-farm out there, with Rubbish the goat, Schumacher the tortoise, all the rabbits and chickens and so on. Children will love it and so will their parents and we'll make lots of money just in time for Christmas. Now try to tell me what's wrong with that?'

Mum folded her arms crossly and sat down in a huff.

I glanced at Dad. He was tugging at his beard and that meant he was thinking very hard.

'Sounds like a pretty good plan to me, Dad,' I offered. He growled and scowled and pointed an accusing finger at Mum.

'I'll tell you something, Brenda,' he began, speaking through gritted teeth. 'This idea of yours, well, all I can say is – IT'S UTTERLY NUTTERLY BRILLIANT! Would you like a dance?'

He grabbed Mum and began to twirl her round the floor. It would have been OK if we weren't in the kitchen, but we were. Within seconds the pair of them had sent two plates crashing to the floor, knocked over the milk and

trodden on Tomato's left foot.

'Waaaaaahh!'

'Oops!' said Dad, gathering my sister into his arms. 'I think we've got a squashed Tomato. Shall I kiss it better for you?'

And do you know what he did? Dad took off her shoe, peeled off her sock AND KISSED HER FOOT! TOTAL YURRKK!

That's disgusting! I'm never going to be a parent when I grow up if you have to do things like that.

Tomato was OK really and Mum gave her some banana to eat. Good trick! She could hardly cry with half a banana in her mouth.

After that we sat down and drew up our master plan. We thought of all the different shapes we could make with gingerbread: Father Christmas, angels, stars, holly leaves, snowmen, space rockets (guess whose idea that was?), snowflakes and chickens (Tomato's idea).

We cleared the kitchen table and covered it with a plastic cloth. Mum got out all the stuff we would need, plus a whole lot more, just in case. Soon one end of the table was piled high with little tubs and jars and packets of this and that. At the other end of the table was another pile of mixing bowls, jugs, spoons, forks, egg whisks and so on.

A deep roar from a motorbike outside announced the arrival of Granny and Lancelot.

Granny came into the kitchen carrying a suitcase.

Dad's face clouded over. 'You're not coming to stay are you?' he gasped.

'Ron, she's your mother!' laughed Mum. She turned to Granny. 'Just ignore him,' she advised.

'Oh I shall,' smiled Granny, offering Dad her cheek. 'Fancy a big boy not wanting his mummy any more. Come on, Ron, give your mummy a big kiss!'

Dad paid no attention. He was still looking at the suitcase suspiciously and wanted to know what was in it.

'Just some old clothes that Lancelot and I don't need any longer. I know you are very short of money and I thought some of these clothes might be useful.' Granny opened up the suitcase and began tugging out jumpers, baggy trousers, patched jackets, flowery hats, giant frilly knickers –

'Mother! We do not wish to

wear your old knickers, thank you very much!'
cried Dad, holding them up in horror. Lancelot
creased up with laughter.

'They're so big I reckon you could get three
grannies in that pair, babe!' he said.

Granny turned very red and she snatched them
back. 'They got in there by mistake. Stop making
such a fuss, Ron. You're embarrassing Nicholas
and the little ones.'

We weren't the least bit embarrassed. It was
Granny! She quickly tried to change the subject
by asking us what we were doing.

'You've got it all set up for something,' she
hinted, eyeing the kitchen table.

Mum had to tell Granny about the biscuits,
and Granny and Lancelot got terribly excited
and asked if they could help too.

'I haven't made gingerbread for years,' said
Granny.

'And I've NEVER made gingerbread,' added
Lancelot.

So we had to let them join us and it was a bit of a squeeze. We only have a small kitchen and whenever anyone wanted to move, everyone else had to shuffle about. It was crazy, but we got to work.

Soon it was like a factory. Everyone was making something. We were rolling out gingerbread, cutting shapes, dropping things on the floor, spilling stuff, not to mention sending clouds of flour into the air from time to time. Our arms were white up to our elbows. The twins had so much flour smudged on their faces

they looked like a pair of ghosts.

We were all working so hard we didn't notice just how much mess we were making. Lancelot started whisking up some icing to put on the finished biscuits when they came out of the oven. I don't think he'd put the beaters in the whisk properly because all of a sudden both the beaters broke loose and went whizzing across the room like a pair of miniature UFOs and half the icing mix went with them.

Dad ducked as one beater twirled past his head, splattering his hair with icing. The other

beater hit the ceiling, stuck there for a few seconds and then dropped straight back down and landed – SPLOP! – on Lancelot's head. It looked like he had an aerial poking out of his skull.

We all stared at him. Lancelot looked carefully at what was left of the whisk he was holding and said, 'It wasn't supposed to do that.'

We spent the next half hour cleaning. Meanwhile the kitchen filled with the smell of baking biscuits – yum yum! When they came out of the oven they looked brilliant.

'Want a bicky!' cried the twins. Well, we all did! And as soon as they were cool enough Mum handed some round.

'The Christmas tree shapes are mine and

the others are Ron's,' she
announced. 'What are they
meant to be, Ron?'

'Snakes.'

'Snakes?' repeated Mum.
'I don't think snakes are very
Christmassy.'

'That's just it,' said Dad. 'I
thought, you never see snakes
at Christmas, do you? Why
should they miss out? So this
year I'm inviting snakes to
take part in Christmas.'

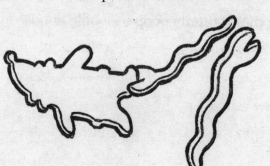

'You're an idiot,' Mum told him.

'Thank you very much,' Dad grinned.

'And I love you because you're an idiot,' Mum went on.

'Oh. That's all right then,' Dad beamed.

So we tried the gingerbread. Mum's was lovely – just right. We tried Dad's too but you have never seen so much coughing and spluttering and rushing to the sink for some cold water and everyone washing out their mouths and the twins starting to cry and generally complete chaos and uproar.

'RON!' yelled Mum. 'Why have you made these biscuits with CURRY POWDER? Ron, come back here! Don't you run away and hide! We'll come and find you! Ron – you nincompoop, you utterly poop-a-doodle noodle-brain. RON!'

4. Here Come the Christmas Vampires

We found him. He was in the double wardrobe in Mum and Dad's bedroom, hiding behind Mum's dresses. He is such a clown!

'It was a mistake,' Dad insisted. 'The tubs of powder must have got mixed up. I sniffed one and it had a nice, strong smell so I thought it must be ginger. I didn't mean to do it,' he added, sounding a bit like me when I was six and had done something wrong.

Mum has now banned him from cooking. 'I don't want any more of your ridiculous curry snakes, thank you very much. You can make some notices to put in local shops to say that we are holding a CHRISTMAS OPEN DAY this weekend. Nicholas and I are going to think about other things to make that we can sell – decorations for the tree and so on.'

'I want to make things too,' Dad complained. 'I like making things.'

'We know,' said Mum. 'There was the Tyrannosaurus slide you made Nicholas when he was seven and now he's thirteen and you still haven't finished it. There's the extra shed you started to build for the garden but it fell down before you could put the roof on. Then there was the climbing frame you built for Cheese and Tomato to play on and it's still only half done. Now it's covered in ivy.'

'It does look pretty when it's in flower,' Dad pointed out.

'Ivy doesn't flower,' Mum said stonily. 'Have you ever noticed how often you don't finish things? I don't want to have a pile of unfinished Christmas decorations that nobody wants to buy.'

'But I've got some cracking ideas,' Dad said.

'Such as?'

'Well, you know how people often put a Christmas fairy on top of their tree? Why is that? Why does it have to be a fairy?' Dad asked.

Mum shook her head. 'Ron, you're not going to suggest we put a Christmas snake on top of the tree, are you?'

Dad took a deep breath as if he was about to say 'yes' and then thought better of it. 'Er, no, but why is it always a fairy? Why can't we have a gnome, or a hobgoblin? What about a Christmas vampire? Fairies are so goody-two-shoes, aren't they?'

'Maybe, but that's what people want at Christmas,' Mum argued. 'Funnily enough they don't often ask for Christmas vampires.'

'They would if they knew where they could get them. I think Christmas vampires would be very popular,' Dad went on. 'In fact, I've thought of something even better. How about we make some little Mr Tuggs and we stick *him* on top of the Christmas tree? That would be brilliant! Mr

Tugg sitting there with –'

'I get the picture,' Mum put in quickly. 'And I think you're being very silly. Go away and write out those notices to put in the shops. Nicholas and the twins and I are going to make sensible Christmas decorations.'

As Dad went from the room he called over his shoulder in a very BORING voice. 'Hope you have fun, Nick, making FAIRIES.'

I have to admit I was not exactly looking forward to it. Christmas vampires – now that sounded a lot better. I suggested it to Mum. 'I could make, say, two and we could see if they sell or not.'

'All right, all right,' Mum gave in. 'But no more than two, and please don't get too much like your Dad.' She shook her head. 'No, it's not possible really. NOBODY could be like your Dad. He's a one-off.'

I think Mum's right!

Cheese and Tomato helped us with the

decorations. Mum gave them bits of ribbon and showed them how to tie the ribbon on so that the decoration could be hung on a tree, or somewhere suitable. That kept the twins busy for a good long while, but the results were not always perfect.

Most of Tomato's angels were dangling upside down because she had strung them up by the leg!

Mum looked at the upside-down angels in amazement.

'What is it with this house? Or is it something about the people who live in it? Why on earth are they the wrong way up?'

This was Tomato's brilliant answer. 'They're from Ossylala. My teacher says Ossylala is on the other side of the world and the world is round and we're on the top bit and if you walk all the way round to the bottom you'd be upside down, wouldn't you? So the angels in Ossylala must be upside down too.'

If you haven't guessed, Ossylala is Tomato's way of saying Australia. Meanwhile, Cheese had been tying his ribbons to a pile of Father Christmases. He'd tied them round the belly!

I think Mum just gave up in despair at that point. She went back to the kitchen to be on her own. While she was gone I made as many Christmas vampires as I could. It was great fun. I decorated them with bits of silver glitter and tinsel to put them in the Christmas mood. I only left two on the table and I hid the rest. I don't know what I'm going to do with them. Maybe I can sell them at school later.

Dad disappeared outside clutching a pile of notices to put up. He was out for a couple of hours. This is what they said:

FANTASTIC OPEN DAY!
COME AND SEE YOUR LOCAL MODEL FARM IN ACTION.

CHICKENS! GOAT! RABBITS! TORTOISE! ELEPHANTS!

TEA, COFFEE, DRINKS, CAKES, BISCUITS

PLUS

EXCLUSIVE CHRISTMAS DECORATIONS!

ENTRANCE 50p

Mum checked it through when he got back. She went to the back door, peered into the garden for a minute or two and came back.

'What's up?' asked Dad.

'I was looking for the elephants. You've told everyone that we have elephants in our back garden. So where are they?'

'Well, of course they're not there *yet*,' said Dad. 'But they will be.'

'Really? Where are you going to get elephants from?' Mum demanded.

'Cheese has some. He's got three model elephants in his play zoo. I am going to put them in the garden.' Dad smiled triumphantly.

'They're so small nobody will see them,' said Mum.

'Exactly. In fact I am going to hide them. If someone manages to find one of them they'll get a prize – like a Christmas vampire. Something special.'

'You know, Ron, sometimes you surprise me.

Sometimes you can really be quite clever. That's a good idea – except for the Christmas vampire. Nobody will want one of those. We'll give them a special packet of gingerbread Christmas shapes instead.'

So everything is sweetness and light in our house once more. We are all set for our Grand Open Day tomorrow. We're going to have a big tidy-up first thing, indoors and out.

Granny and Lancelot are coming over to help. They'll be here on the Open Day too, helping to make drinks and serve them from the kitchen. Mum wants me to be a waiter and Dad will be out in the garden keeping an eye on the animals to make sure they behave themselves.

I think Dad might need to behave too!

5. A Weapon of Mass Destruction

Did I say Dad would be making sure the animals behaved themselves? Ha ha ha! I must have been joking. Well, actually I *wasn't* joking but things didn't work out as we had hoped. I guess I'd better tell you.

Lancelot and Granny arrived first thing in the morning carrying a bulging bag of old clothes.

'You could sell these as jumble,' suggested Granny. 'Anything to make an extra penny or two.'

'That's kind of you,' said Mum. 'What a good idea.'

Dad pulled another extremely large pair of knickers out of the bag. 'Mother, I don't think ANYONE will want to buy THESE!'

Granny wagged a finger at him. 'You'd be

surprised at what people buy sometimes. And stop waving them around like that, you're embarrassing Nicholas. Look, his face is like a traffic light on STOP. Now then, how can we help?'

'There's so much tidying up and sorting to do,' Mum told her, so Granny began bustling about. She picked up things that Mum wanted, like a special bowl – that sort of thing – and put it away somewhere. Then Mum would spend half an hour looking for the bowl she thought was on the table and would

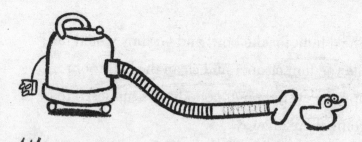

eventually discover it where Granny had put it. Then Mum would go to get the vacuum cleaner from the cupboard and find it wasn't there because Granny had used it in the hall and hadn't put it back. While looking for the vacuum cleaner Mum would put the bowl back on the table.

While Mum searched for the vacuum cleaner, Granny would see the bowl on the table, shake her head and put it away again. Mum would return with the vacuum cleaner only to find the bowl gone.

She'd hunt for the bowl and Granny would take the vacuum cleaner and clean the bathroom upstairs even though nobody was supposed to be going there anyway.

There was a lot of shouting going on between them, mostly up and down the stairs or from one room to another.

'Have you seen the blue bowl?' Mum would yell.

'The poo mole?' Granny would answer. She's a bit deaf sometimes and doesn't hear things properly. 'I didn't know you had a mole. What did you get a mole for and why –?'

'No! The BLUE BOWL!'

'A BLUE mole? I've never heard of a –'

'BLUE B – O – W– L!' Mum would spell out.

'No need to shout, dear, I'm not deaf.'

'Yes you are!' Mum replied.

'What did you say?' Granny would ask, and then Mum would have to let off steam.

'Aaaaaargh!'

All this time Cheese and Tomato were 'helping'. That mostly meant getting in the way and stealing cakes from the kitchen, but at least they were enjoying themselves. Amazingly, things slowly began to take shape. The table in the dining room was piled high with scones and gingerbread. We cleared a bookshelf in the front room and set out all the

Christmas decorations on it. We spread Granny's jumble on a folding table.

The kitchen was the real centre of operations. Granny and Lancelot had brought round all their cups and saucers and plates so that there would be enough for all the visitors we were expecting. There were no less than three kettles ready to boil up water and the fridge was stuffed with milk, butter and cream, ready for the teas.

Out in the garden Dad had managed to wash Rubbish using the hose and some shampoo. Washing goats is a bit tricky because they jump about a lot, ram you with their head and kick you with their back feet. So Dad also managed to wash the back wall of the house, the kitchen door, most of the windows, a bit of the roof, a lot of himself and Mr Tugg's face.

That last bit was a mistake. Dad hadn't meant to wash Mr Tugg's face but Mr Tugg stuck his head out of his back door at just the wrong moment and got the hose up his nose.

'Sorry!' cried Dad.

'Spllllrrrgrgh!' yelped Mr Tugg, very wetly.

Still, Rubbish looked sparkly clean by the time
Dad had finished. So did Mr Tugg's head.

Two o'clock in the afternoon was opening
time and THERE WAS A QUEUE! People
came pouring through the front door, where
Lancelot was charging them fifty pence to get
in. The crowds came pounding down the hall,
spilling into the downstairs rooms and out into
the garden. Dad was suddenly overwhelmed with
shouting parents and their even noisier children.

'Oh look – rabbits! There's a rabbit. Look at the rabbit, Taylor. Taylor, look at the rabbit!'

'Look, LOOK! A hippo!'

'No, Trixibell, that's a goat,' said Trixibell's mother. Trixibell wanted to know what goats ate and held out her hand towards Rubbish.

'Goats will eat anything,' Dad explained, just as Rubbish stuck out her long tongue, licked Trixibell's hand from top to bottom and then tried to swallow it.

'She's eating my arm!' complained Trixibell, while her brother, Jayden, fixed Dad with a sneer

and bet my dad that goats wouldn't eat a nuclear
bomb.

'Or a planet,' Jayden went on. 'Or a house,
or a space ship, or a car, or the Empire State
Building, or a whole island with trees on it and
everything, or a Tyrannosaurus rex, or a black
hole, or a –'

'I think I've got the general idea,' Dad
muttered wearily. 'Why don't you see if Rubbish
can eat your head?'

'I heard that,' scowled Jayden's father. He lifted
his eyebrows and squinted at my dad. Then he
added in a rather thoughtful tone that it might be
a good idea, and smiled.

Inside the house the teas were selling like hot
cakes. Although, actually, the hot cakes were
selling like hot cakes and the tea was selling like,
well, tea. The decorations we'd made were being
snapped up too.

And guess what? My Christmas vampires were
sold IMMEDIATELY! I whizzed upstairs and

got out the extra ones I'd hidden away and those sold in seconds too. Result! But the funniest thing was the jumble. There was this very loud woman who looked as if someone had tipped a lorry-load of hay on top of her head but it was all her own hair – amazing! Anyhow, she was going through the jumble and she pulled out Granny's giant knickers and BOUGHT THEM!

I couldn't help asking her what she was going to do with them.

'Oh, I'm going to sew up the leg holes and I shall knit a pair of colourful handles and they'll make a lovely shopping bag.'

Aren't people crazy?!

The whole afternoon was going brilliantly. Even Mr and Mrs Tugg had come round to join in. Mrs Tugg is a very large, wobbly lady. She laughs a lot so you do rather notice the wobbling. It starts with her chins and goes right the way down her body. It looks as if there's someone inside her shaking very hard. I like Mrs Tugg.

She's much friendlier than her fire-cracker husband.

Mr Tugg had come in his latest hat. He often wears hats in the winter. I guess his bald head gets cold. He was sporting a smart, check-patterned flat cap. He kept tweaking the front of it. I think he was hoping that people would notice. He sat at the back of the dining room, with a cup of tea and a cream-filled scone, scowled like mad and tweaked his hat at everyone.

Everything was going pretty well and we were almost at the end of the afternoon when disaster struck, and the disaster was goat-shaped.

It wasn't really Rubbish's fault. A man brought his dog. That was pretty brainless for a start, and it wasn't just the man who was brainless. The dog didn't have a brain either. You don't take dogs to a place where small animals are running around. OK, so Rubbish may not be all that small, but hens and rabbits are. I've no idea how the man managed to get the dog past Lancelot.

It was a big dog too. A
big stupid dog. As soon as it
saw the rabbits the dog was
off. It pulled the man right
over, into the mud. Served
him right too, but he let
go of the lead, didn't he?
The dog went zooming off
and the rabbits scattered in

every direction, which is hardly surprising.

Now everyone in the garden was screaming and shouting. The rabbits were whizzing round tripping everyone up. The dog went galumphing after them, knocking people over as if they were skittles, and that set Rubbish off.

The goat took one look at the big black hairy thing thundering towards her and leaped straight out of her pen. She went charging down the garden path, through the kitchen and into the dining room. She only came to a halt when she crashed into Mr Tugg's table, upsetting all the cream and milk into his lap and causing his hat to fall off.

He tried to jump up but couldn't because the table had trapped his legs.

That was when Rubbish ate Mr Tugg's new hat. I think she liked the green bits best. They probably reminded her of grass. Mr Tugg wasn't happy. He did a volcano AND firework imitation all in one go. It was pretty impressive. And noisy.

Dad came wading through the mess after Rubbish and hauled her back outside. By this time people were trying to escape and leaving fast. Most of them had something to complain about – clothes covered in jam, or mud, or cream, or cake – maybe even the whole lot.

Jayden's father had torn his trousers. He eyed Dad and Rubbish on the way out. 'You should sell that goat to the army,' he advised. 'She's a weapon of mass destruction.'

6. Some Unwrapped Cheese

GLOOM. It's been like a rainstorm in our house, only without the rain – just the doom and gloom. This morning there were about ten envelopes on the doormat. They all had bills inside from people who had got damaged clothes from our Open Day. There were bills for cleaning, bills for repairing and some people had had to buy brand-new clothes and wanted us to pay for those too.

We'd made a lovely little pile of money for Christmas from all our hard work. Now most of it would have to go towards paying people for the trouble caused by Mr Idiot and his idiot dog.

'We're back to square one,' moaned Dad. 'Now what do we do? We can't hold another Open Day. It was our one chance of rescuing Christmas and it's gone.'

'Something will turn up,' said Mum, but she looked pretty uncertain about it.

I tried hard to think of some clever plan that would make us oodles of money and put a smile on everybody's faces. I couldn't bear it. It was even worse when I overheard Cheese and Tomato talking to each other.

'I'm getting a rocket for Christmas,' Cheese told his sister. 'And it's as big, as big, as big as a WHALE!'

'Can I come in your rocket?' asked Tomato.

'Hmm. But you'll have to sit at the back because I'm driving.'

'Will we go to the shops?'

'No. You don't go shopping in a rocket. You go to Space,' replied Cheese.

'Oh. Does Space have shops?' said Tomato.

Cheese went quiet. I wondered what he would say. He was thinking hard. Were there shops in space? If there weren't then where would they get their food?

'Hmm,' he said eventually. 'There are shops on some of the stars.'

'Do they have parking?' asked Tomato. I almost laughed out loud. Mum and Dad are ALWAYS looking for a parking space when we go shopping. Dad usually ends up shouting at people.

I never got to hear Cheese's answer because at that point the doorbell rang. You will never guess who it was – someone from our past, someone quite large and very cheerful.

'Jack Dumper!' cried Mum, giving him a hug and a kiss. 'What are you doing HERE?'

'Hey!' said Dad, trying to sound cross, but actually grinning from ear to ear. He tapped Mum on the shoulder. 'Put that man down at once!' And he shook Mr Dumper's hand.

Here's a quick bit about Jack Dumper. He's the boss of a big company that makes disposable, eco-friendly nappies. When Cheese was very small he appeared in a famous advert for the nappies. Even more famously, Cheese appeared on the national news! He was on TV, crawling across the newsreader's desk with no clothes on! That's how he got his famous bottom!

But Cheese is much too old to do any more nappy advertisements, so why was Jack Dumper standing on our doorstep?

'OK, here's the info,' Mr Dumper began. 'I'm branching out. We're not just making nappies any more. We're going into children's clothing. Got a whole new range of snazzy stuff – gonna call the range JUMPA-DUMPS.'

'Jumpa-Dumps?' repeated Dad. 'That's a catchy name. But why go into making kiddies' clothes?'

Mr Dumper smiled. 'You remember when Cheese got on TV by mistake and half the nation saw his bottom? Of course you do. Well, recently there was a programme on TV where they asked people to choose their funniest film clips. You know what?'

Mum gasped. 'Cheese won?'

Jack laughed and shook his head. 'No, but almost – he came third! Imagine that. Thousands of people chose that film clip as their funniest and favourite one. That got me thinking. Cheese is already a star. So why not use Cheese – and Tomato – in a new ad campaign? Only this time it won't be nappies, it will be young kiddies' clothes. And that's how Jumpa-Dumps was born.

'I want Cheese and Tomato to be my models for a lot of the clothes. We'll do a big photoshoot. It'll be in all the best magazines, maybe on TV too. Cheese and Tomato will be the face of Jumpa-Dumps when we launch just in time for Christmas. And of course you'll all get paid for whatever work you do. What do you think?'

Mum looked at Dad. Dad looked at Mum. I looked at both of them. They looked at me.

I looked at Cheese and Tomato. They looked at each other. There was an awful lot of looking.

'I think,' Dad began, 'I think we should open a bottle of champagne!'

'Shame we haven't got one,' chuckled Mum.

Mr Dumper nodded. 'I've got one in the fridge in my car. I was hoping you'd agree. I'll go and fetch it right now.'

Dad and I looked at each other. Our eyes were on stalks. *Mr Dumper had a FRIDGE in his CAR?!!*

Wow!

7. It's Raining Indoors!

MAD DAY! It's been completely bonker-loony.
It started with the twins arguing.

'Uncle Jack is going to take us into space,'
Cheese told his sister.

'He's got a CAR,' Tomato answered flatly.
'Cars can't fly and they can't go into space.'

'Yes they can if they have rockets,' Cheese
replied. 'They can go whoosh and they go up and
up and up higher than Mount Everest and then
they're in space.'

'And you haven't got a space suit and you'll
die,' Tomato went on unhelpfully.

Cheese would have none of it. 'I'll have space
socks and space shoes and space pants and space
trousers and a space top and space gloves and a
space helmet and I won't die.'

Tomato chewed this over for a few seconds. 'And anyway it's boring in space and you can only ever eat sandwiches because you can't cook and anyway you can't see anything because it's dark as dark as dark.'

Cheese smiled triumphantly. 'Well, YOU won't see anything because YOU'RE NOT COMING WITH ME! SO THERE – NURR!'

The twins happily quarrelled away while the rest of us got ready for the first fashion shoot. Mr Dumper had arranged for a car to come and collect us. All he had told us was that the twins would be modelling a range of clothes for winter

and another range for summer.

Cheese pulled anxiously at my leg. 'Tomato says we won't see anything in space because it's dark.'

'I'll lend you my torch,' I told him and he happily beetled off to tell his sister.

The car took ages to arrive. That was because the front part of it seemed to arrive hours before the back part. The car was SO LONG! It was a white stretch limo. It seemed to take up most of our street.

It had a proper chauffeur too, with a uniform and a peaked cap. He came marching up our

drive but before he could reach our door he was ambushed by Mr Tugg.

'You're parked across my drive,' grumbled Mr Tugg.

'Yes, sir,' the chauffeur began politely. 'In fact, I'm parked across three people's drives but I shall be gone in five minutes.'

'But I can't get out,' snapped Mr Tugg.

'I shall be gone in a jiffy, sir.'

'But suppose I want to go right now?' demanded Mr Tugg. 'It could be an emergency. I might be expecting a baby.'

The chauffeur looked at Mr Tugg's belly and then at his face. 'I don't think you're pregnant, sir, and, as I said, I shall be gone very soon. In fact, if we could stop talking I could knock on this door and we would be able to go straight away.'

Mr Tugg bristled. 'Aha! I knew it would be something to do with them. They're nothing but trouble, you know. I wouldn't let them in your car for one moment. They'll very likely fill it with water and put a shark in it.' Mr Tugg was beginning to go red. He was on the edge of becoming a volcano.

The chauffeur eyed Mr Tugg curiously. 'Why would anyone put a shark in a car?' he asked.

'That's what my neighbours are like,' growled Mr Tugg. 'They're completely crackers. They put an alligator in my car once. They've got a goat that eats hats. And their chickens make your bottom go spotty.'

The chauffeur didn't say a word, but his mouth opened and shut a lot as if he was struggling to think of what to say to all this.

'And now you are all blocking my drive,' Mr Tugg repeated.

The chauffeur was quite a lot taller than Mr Tugg, so he reached over Mr Tugg's shoulder and rang our doorbell. Dad opened the door.

'Your car, sir,' announced the chauffeur.

'You're blocking my drive!' shouted Mr Tugg.

'We're all ready,' Dad said, and we trooped out of the house and piled into the limo while the chauffeur held open the door for us. I felt like a film star! It was brilliant.

'You're blocking my drive!' yelled Mr Tugg again as the chauffeur closed the door and went to the driver's seat. The engine purred into life and we slowly moved off. Mr Tugg hammered on the windows but we could no longer hear what he was saying.

And then we were off, gliding down the road

and lying back in seats almost as big as beds – huge, comfortable, sink-down-for-miles beds.

I looked out of the rear window and saw Mr Tugg still jumping up and down in the middle of the road. He was in full volcano mode, his little arms pumping and steam coming out of his ears. Poor Mr Tugg. Sometimes I feel quite sorry for him. I mean, what's the point in getting so worked up? I guess some people are just like that.

I didn't want our journey to end. It was absolutely fabulous drifting along in that limo. We opened up all the little cupboards and it was like having a mini Christmas in the car.

'There are packets of nuts in here!' I cried.

'There are drinks in here – oh my, it's a fridge, and it's got chocolate too!' sighed Mum.

'Chocolate, please,' Tomato and Cheese chorused.

'I don't believe it. Look at this,' said Dad. He opened two little doors and there was a wash basin with taps and a plug and soap and a little

towel. Then we found the television and computer. One set of seats even folded down into a proper bed. Talk about luxury! This was the bizz!

But where were we going? At that moment the telephone rang. Telephone? In the car? Dad answered.

'Helllooooo,' he said in a funny voice, and we all tried not to laugh.

It was Jack Dumper, phoning to explain that we were on our way to the Palm House at Kew Gardens in London. Jack wanted Cheese and Tomato to model the summer clothing collection there.

'It's where they keep dozens of tropical plants like palm trees and so on,' Jack told Dad. 'It will be a stunning setting for photographing the summer collection.'

Have you ever been to the Palm House at Kew? It is HUGE. I mean it is just WHAM BAM MEGA GINORMOUS and made of glass. The inside is simply full of plants – and heat.

THE HEAT! It almost knocks you off your feet and it makes you feel all clammy and sweaty. The leaves on those plants are as big as umbrellas. Some of them had massive flowers that you could practically climb into. I kept expecting to see fat slinky snakes sliding among the leaves and zany parrots flitting from one branch to another, not to mention Tarzan. You'd have thought he'd come swinging across at any moment:

'*AI-EEE AI-EEEE AI-EEEE!*'

In fact there was nobody there at all apart from the photo people and Jack Dumper. He had paid to have the whole place for a few hours. The photographers began to set up their cameras while Cheese and Tomato were whisked off to get changed into the summer clothes.

Cheese reappeared wearing some long red swim shorts with monkeys climbing all over them. (Not real monkeys – I mean pictures of monkeys!) Tomato's costume was covered with colourful butterflies. (No, not real butterflies!)

I suddenly felt a stab of envy. They seemed to be having so much fun and getting all the attention. I was only there because they couldn't

exactly leave me at home on my own. I felt like I was just an extra babysitter.

To tell you the truth I was getting a bit bored by it all. Fashion shoots are mostly waiting around while the photographers fiddle with their cameras and check the lighting and all that stuff. I went wandering off and found the tree-top walkway. That was much more interesting, especially when it rained.

IT WASN'T SUPPOSED TO RAIN! WE WERE INDOORS!

Let me tell you how it happened. I was pretty high up, almost in the tree-tops. I was wandering along quite happily when I felt a few spots of water, and then some more. Soon it was pouring. I didn't get all that wet because I was above most of it, but down below me it was like being in a tropical storm. Water was pouring down just like a real rainstorm. Every day the plants had to be watered. So every day the sprinkler system

came on and automatically watered everything and everywhere – and that included anyone who happened to be inside.

Screams came from below. Shouts and yells and people racing all over the place, quickly hiding their cameras from the rain. Eventually a gardener heard the cries coming from the Palm House and turned off the water.

By this time Jack, Mum, Dad, everyone – they were all soaked. I came down from the walkway pretty much dry.

'Was that you, Nicholas?' Mum demanded sternly.

I was speechless. All I'd done was wander among the tree-tops. It turned out that one of the gardeners had seen that nobody was going into the Palm House. He thought it was a good time to give the plants a watering and had turned on the sprinkler system.

Mr Dumper was seething. 'That's the whole photoshoot ruined. We'll have to do it all again tomorrow!'

8. I'm in Heaven

It was already late afternoon so Mr Dumper sent us to a hotel. Actually, it wasn't just any hotel, it was a ten-star hotel. You should have seen it. Swanky, or what! There were loads of mega-expensive cars parked outside – two Ferraris, a Rolls Royce, three Bentleys, a Lamborghini and an Aston Martin. Wow!

I stroked the Aston and whispered to Dad, 'Do

you think James Bond is staying here?' He smiled and we all squelched into the hotel, dripping from our heads, noses, ears, chins, elbows and knees. We left little puddles behind with every step, right across the lobby of the hotel. You'll never guess what my dad did. He walked up to the reception desk, looked at the girl behind the desk straight in the eye and growled at her.

'You have a room for me. The name's Bond, James Bond. I'll have a cup of tea on the rocks, shaken but not spilled.'

The girl's face crumpled into a worried mess. 'I beg your pardon, sir? Can I help you?'

Dad leaned forward and several drops of water splopped off his nose and on to the desk. 'I'm in disguise,' he murmured. '007, licensed to get very wet.'

Mum pushed Dad heavily to one side. 'Please ignore my husband,' she said coldly. 'We are guests of Jack Dumper.'

The worried face of the girl turned into a

bright smile and she clutched at her heart with relief. 'Oh! Your husband was making a joke!'

Mum sighed. 'You could call it that,' she agreed. 'But jokes are meant to be funny, aren't they?'

The girl laughed and said Mr Dumper had warned her we'd been caught in a shower. She gave us our room number and keys. Room 2205. 'It's on the twenty-second floor,' the girl explained.

I gulped. Twenty-second floor?

We got into the lift and when it started with a quiet *whooosh* Cheese really, really

thought we were going into space.

We reached our room and opened the door. You know what? It wasn't one room at all. It was SIX ROOMS! They were:

1. Great big lounge area with the most gigantic wall-to-wall, floor-to-ceiling window looking out over the entire WORLD! (Well, that's what it seemed like.) And all the Christmas lights were beginning to come on way down below, sparkling like tiny jewels all over the city.
2. Bathroom, with a bath on brass lion's paws right in the middle, and the bath was almost as big as a swimming pool.
3. A room just for clothes – NOT a wardrobe, a whole ROOM, just for hanging clothes. Mum said it was the Dressing Room.

4. A bedroom for Mum and Dad. I didn't know which way to lie on their bed, it was so enormous, and really comfortable, with hundreds of cushions. There was also another giant window looking at the world.

5. Cheese and Tomato's room, with two big beds and their own telly and own little shower and toilet and everything.

6. MY BEDROOM with a DOUBLE BED the size of a PLANET. And I had my own bathroom to the side and toilet and everything.

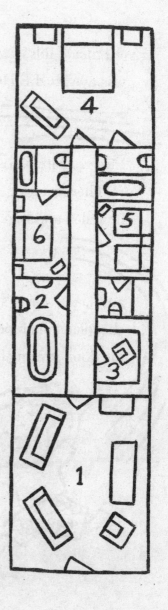

I mean, this wasn't a room in a hotel – this was a WHOLE HOUSE IN A HOTEL! Cheese

came rushing into my room.

'There's a fridge in our room with chocolate!' he yelled and went zooming straight out to Mum

and Dad. 'There's a fridge in our room with chocolate!' he repeated, before racing over to the door, sticking his head out into the corridor and yelling excitedly, 'We've got a fridge in our room with CHOCOLATE!'

By this time I was investigating my fridge too. There it all was – the chocolate, biscuits, crisps, fruit, drinks – the whole lot. Now I knew for sure that I wasn't in a hotel at all.

I was in Heaven!

We were all pretty tired. We'd had the excitement of the limo AND been caught in a tropical rainstorm in the middle of London. It had all been mighty strange. Mum decided that we would order breakfast to come to our room in the morning and we should all go to sleep. I could hardly wait to climb into my luxury bed and I slept like a log.

I had a weird dream where Mum asked me to help her make a Christmas cake. I didn't want to help because, as you know, I HATE Christmas cake. Anyhow, I went to the cupboard to get some flour. It was on a high shelf. I reached up and managed to get the bag in my fingers but it tipped over. It began spilling down over my head but it wasn't flour at all, it was water!

The water kept pouring over me. Soon it came up to my shins and then right up to my knees and

still it was sheeting down. I heard a distant yodel
– *AI-EEE AI-EEEE AI-EEEE!* It was Tarzan,
swinging through the trees wearing a red bikini!
He let go of the rope and dived into the raging
water. The next moment I was standing on
Tarzan's back and he was like a surfboard on the
raging river.

I was riding Tarzan, with the wind racing through my hair. Then Dad was coming up fast behind me in a huge limo, trying to overtake me. He had a sort of big slingshot and he kept firing Christmas cakes at me, missing me mostly until one Christmas cake got me, SPLABBAPP! on my side. I fell off and got rolled over and over by the

waves, struggling to get out of the water, but I was trapped.

I woke with a jolt. I'd got the bed sheets wound round and round me and I was lying on the floor! I'd managed to fall out of bed. What a nightmare! Phew. I was so pleased to be awake.

It took me a few moments to remember where I was and then it all came rushing back. THE HOTEL! Yippee! Time for a mega-sonic bath in my very own mega-sonic bathtub. It was big enough for a rhinoceros. Honk-honk, SPERRLASH! (That's a rhino getting into my bath.)

There were all these little freebies in the bathroom – shampoo, soap, shower gel, bubble bath, all sorts. I set the tap running and poured in some bubble bath.

I think I must have put in a bit too much. Before I knew it there was foam creeping up over the edge of the bath and slopping down on to the floor. Oops! Pretty cool though! I dived in, sank beneath the bubbles and turned into Godzilla, the

foaming monster – rising, roaring from the depths
to challenge the world.

RAAAAAAAARRGGHHH!

That was when the hotel maid came in,
screamed, and dropped my breakfast tray on the
floor.

**KERRASH! SKRANNGGG! SHATTER!
BLOOP-BLOOP-BLOOP!**

Oh dear. Double oops! That certainly scrambled my eggs. Why hadn't she knocked before she came in? (Answer: She had knocked but I was under all that foam and didn't hear so she thought the room was empty.)

Never mind. She soon recovered and ran off to get some more breakfast. (Plus a mop and bucket.)

So, what with the nightmare AND the maid, the day didn't start too well. Hopefully it could only get better.

9. A Bit of Zap!

'There's been a change of plan,' Jack Dumper told us. 'As you know, yesterday's photoshoot was ruined by the unexpected downpour. I wanted to re-book the Palm House at Kew but there's a special Christmas event going on there today. So we move on to Plan B. We're going to shoot the winter clothes collection instead.'

'Sounds good to me,' I nodded. 'Are we going in the limo again?'

'We certainly are,' Jack said.

I glanced across at Dad. 'Just leave the Christmas cake slingshot behind, Dad, OK?'

Poor Dad. He looked totally puzzled so I had to tell everyone about my dream. They fell about laughing, especially when I found myself on the floor with the sheet wrapped round me.

I didn't even get any sympathy from Cheese and Tomato.

'You're silly,' Tomato told me.

'Silly-billy,' hooted Cheese. 'Silly-billy-spilly!' He thought that was so incredibly funny he repeated it about ten times, laughing so much he got the hiccups. Well, he is only four.

We all piled into the limo – and I do mean ALL of us – Mum, Dad, Cheese and Tomato, me, Jack Dumper and two photographers, one make-up artist and three assistants. That's

twelve people, plus the driver. Thirteen. I told you it was a big stretch limo. It was so big it even had a garden shed. (Just joking!)

We drove slowly through the London streets, which were full of Christmas shoppers. I could see them trying to stare through the darkened windows of the limo to see who was inside. I bet they thought it was somebody famous. I certainly *felt* famous!

Eventually we arrived at an indoor ski centre. It was one of those proper ones too with artificial

snow sprinkled all over it so it looked just like the real thing.

Not only that, but the whole place had been decorated for Christmas. The ski lifts going up the side of the long ski run had been hung with Christmas lights and tinsel. There was a huge fat red plastic Father Christmas standing at the bottom of the slope going 'HO! HO! HO!' every time somebody went past. Up and down the slope there were big plastic reindeer with shiny

noses, laughing elves and lots of little artificial Christmas trees with twinkly lights. It was all very itty-pretty.

The rows of seats on both sides of the slope were rapidly filling with people, which seemed a little strange, and Mum asked Mr Dumper why there were so many seats either side of the ski run.

'Sometimes they hold ski races here,' he explained, while the twins were taken away to be dressed.

'They're not racing today, are

they?' asked Mum. 'I thought you were going to do a photoshoot here.'

'Oh, we are,' smiled Jack. 'The people sitting down aren't here to see a race. They've come for the fashion show.'

Mum's jaw dropped. 'You mean – the winter collection? Cheese? Tomato? It's an actual *show*?'

'You bet. I realized it would be a brilliant way of getting the shoot done *and* launching the clothes to the press. Most of these people are from newspapers and television.' Jack beamed at us. 'Take a look at the top of the ski run.'

We glanced up. At the very top of the slope was a huge screen. It flickered for a moment as it lit up and there, crawling across the screen, was Cheese, aged one, wearing nothing but a little vest. It was the famous clip from the national news.

'Aw, he's so cute!' cried one woman in the audience.

'I remember seeing that when it happened,'

said a man behind her. 'I laughed so much I spat my coffee halfway across the table!'

At that moment Cheese and Tomato appeared.

'Hey!' cried the coffee-spitting man. 'That's him! That's the kid. Only up there on screen he's unwrapped!' The audience fell about laughing and settled down to watch the fashion show.

The twins looked fantastic. They both wore fur-lined boots that came halfway up their shins and baggy trousers with matching, fur-lined

jackets. They just looked so snug! Tomato had
her hood pulled up and she looked like a goblin
in a winter wonderland.

'We want to photograph you coming down the
slope on a toboggan,' explained Jack. 'Nicholas,
you help them up at the top of the slope and Ron
and Brenda, you catch them at the bottom.'

I took the twins and we climbed on to a ski lift.
It swung and wobbled and the twins giggled all
the way up to the top, where we found several
toboggans neatly lined up. I plonked Cheese and

Tomato on a toboggan and set them off, whizzing down to Mum and Dad. Cameras flashed, the audience clapped and cheered, while the twins were whisked off and put into their next costumes.

'We need a bit more zap,' Jack said. 'The photos are good but not good enough.'

'Zap?' repeated Dad.

'Yes – zap – that little something extra that makes a good shot a great shot,' said Mr Dumper.

'Right,' murmured Dad. I could tell he had no idea what '*zap*' was. Neither did I.

'OK, back to the top and let's try the next lot,' suggested Jack, as Cheese and Tomato came back from the costume change. 'Nicholas, why don't you and your father come down on toboggans at the same time? I think that will look better.'

Wow, I was going to be in the photo too!

You should have seen Dad trying to get on the ski lift! He made such a mess of it. He got

his arms and legs completely tangled and ended
up draped over the seat like a beach towel, with
his legs hanging over one edge and his head and
arms hanging over the other. What's more, all
of this was being shown to the audience on the
BIG SCREEN. They were almost screaming with
laughter as Dad waggled his legs and shouted

'Help!' just as if he were in a cartoon.

At the top Dad popped

Cheese and Tomato

on a toboggan. He pushed them off and as he did
he stepped back, tripped on the toboggan behind
him, sat down heavily on it and the next thing he
was going down the slope too, backwards.

I leaped on to a third toboggan and set off after
him, thinking that maybe I could help. The crowd
laughed and cheered, while Cheese and Tomato
waved and giggled and charmed everyone.

Meanwhile, behind them, there was a crazy
chaotic chase going on. Dad was weaving about
all over the place, almost falling off. His toboggan
skidded everywhere, knocking over reindeer,
trailing little Christmas trees behind it
and running over the poor elves.

I came swooshing behind him, trying to avoid getting clubbed by the reindeer that Dad had sent flying, not to mention assorted elves.

'HELLLPPPPP!' went Dad, as he went faster and faster down the slope, just managing to hold on.

'I'll save you, Dad!' I yelled, totally hopelessly. I had no idea what I could do. And then a reindeer finally knocked him off. He rolled over and over, right down the ski run, cartwheeling and yelling until –

BLABBA-DAMMMMM!

Dad went spinning and crashing straight into the back of Father Christmas. He smashed right through the plastic shell, toppling over the giant Santa so that it ended up rolling gently backwards and forwards in the snow going 'HO! HO! HO!' and 'HELP!' at the same time, but in two different voices.

The crowd were on their feet, trying to clap and clutch their sides with laughter at the same

time. Someone helped Dad climb out from
Santa's belly. I slid to a halt and joined everyone.

'I feel giddy,' said Dad, swaying groggily.

'Hey!' Mr Dumper hurried across to us, waving
his arms excitedly. 'Those last shots were perfect.
The twins looked fab and all that crazy stuff
going on behind them – you should see the shots!
They are brilliant!'

'Was that – "zappy"?' asked Dad, wearily.
Are you happy?'

Jack Dumper threw an arm round Dad's shoulders. 'Ron, I have to tell you that you, YOU are a natural –'

'Clown?' suggested Mum, from behind.

'I was going to say "performer", but I guess it's much the same,' laughed Jack. 'Anyhow, that was the best fashion show I have ever seen. Congratulations, everyone.'

That put a smile on Dad's face. He stood up taller, lifted his chin and beamed at everyone. 'I knew that idea of mine would work. All we needed was a bit of zap and those toboggans are the zappiest I've come across!'

10. Mr Tugg Gets RUDE!

We've all been on the news now, not just Cheese. Half the audience at the ski centre were filming the show on their mobile phones when Dad careered down the slope. It was all a bit like a dream, only it was much nicer than that nightmare I had.

Something even more extraordinary happened to Dad. He got a phone call and he was on the phone for hours. At least it seemed like hours. All we could hear was Dad saying 'yes' every so often, or 'no'. Sometimes he said 'really?' in the kind of voice that makes you think something very interesting is being said at the other end of the line.

By the time Dad put the phone down the whole of the family were listening in at the door – Mum,

Cheese, Tomato and me too.

'What on earth was all that about?' asked Mum.

Dad smiled, and his smile got bigger and bigger and bigger until his face almost split in half. (I'm glad it didn't!)

'I've got a new job,' he announced.

'Never!' cried Mum.

Dad nodded. 'It's true – a new job, at the Ski Centre.'

'THE SKI CENTRE???!!!' we all shouted.

Why would they want to give a job to Dad? He had almost destroyed the place.

'You won't believe this,' Dad began. 'They have asked me to work as a demonstrator to show people how they must not come down the ski slope like I did! I have to show people how NOT to do it! And they'll pay me too! Apparently I'm famous.'

'You remember those people at the fashion show filming me on their mobile phones? Well, that film of me being an idiot is now a big hit on the Internet. Millions of people have seen it. They want to see more of me. The Ski Centre people reckon I have brought them hundreds of new customers and lots of them want to meet the real me. So there you are – you children have got a famous dad!' Dad turned and grinned at Mum. 'And you've got a famous husband!'

Mum looked at him and began shaking. I was a bit worried at first but then I realized she was shaking with laughter. She pointed at Dad – at least she tried to but she was quivering too much.

'Mr Famous! I don't believe it! But that is wonderful news. I am so proud of you. Now we can have the best Christmas ever.'

And it was the best Christmas too, although Cheese didn't get the space ship he wanted. He decided that riding a toboggan was far better than going into space so Dad set about making one for the twins.

'Are you sure that's a good idea?' asked Mum.

'Why shouldn't it be?' Dad answered, a bit prickly.

'I was just remembering when you made Nicholas a kart.'

'So?' Dad said, hammering away at the toboggan.

'The wheels fell off as soon as he sat on it,' Mum reminded him.

'That was because he was so fat,' sniped Dad.

'Dad! I was NOT fat. I have never been fat.'

'All right, you weren't fat but you were wearing

something very heavy. You must have been.
I expect you had an elephant in your pocket.
Something like that.'

Mum and I just looked at him. Dad grinned
and put the hammer down. 'All right. We'll buy
a toboggan,' he announced. 'We can now, with
the money Mr Dumper paid us. And we'll get the
biggest Christmas tree in the world and we shall
have to cut a hole in the ceiling and in the roof
too. It will poke all the way up into the sky and

have a billion twinkly lights on it and Mr Tugg
will complain and we won't care.'

'What's that?' cried Mr Tugg, suddenly poking
his shiny head over the garden fence.

'Oh nothing – I was just saying that you are
like a little twinkly Christmas light and we all
wish you a very happy Christmas, Mr Tugg,' Dad
said cheerfully.

'Hmm, I see,' muttered Mr Tugg, with a big
frown. Honestly, when he gets cross even his bald
head frowns. 'And happy Christmas to you too.'
He turned to go and then came back again. 'But,
I have to say, I really don't think your little boy
should show his bottom like that on television.'

Mum smiled very sweetly at our neighbour.
'Mr Tugg, Cheese was one year old when that
happened, and it was an accident. It was a very
funny accident too.'

Mr Tugg coughed several times. 'Yes, well,
that's all very well. It may have been an accident,
but it was, hurr–rrumph, *(cough cough splutter*

116

splutter) RUDE!'

Mum smiled again. 'Mr Tugg, that's why people liked it.'

Mr Tugg struggled with this amazing idea. 'Well,' he huffed. 'They jolly well shouldn't. It's, it's, it's – oh PIDDLY-POO!' he exclaimed, before hastily slapping a hand over his mouth and squeaking with horror. 'Now you've got me being rude!' He hurried indoors.

'Happy Christmas!' we shouted after him.

LAUGH YOUR SOCKS OFF WITH

Jeremy STRONG

My Brother's Hot Cross Bottom

Turn the page to read the
fantastically funny
first chapter

1. Inky Potatoes

'What on earth is it?' asked Mum, wrinkling her nose as she stared at the box. She always does that when she's puzzled by something and thinking hard. I don't see why wrinkling your nose helps. I've tried it at school when we have maths but it doesn't work.

Mum bent forward and peered at the big, plastic container. The bottom half was white, the top half clear. On the side was a dial and a switch. An electric plug hung off one corner like a bedraggled tail.

Dad stood there, hands on his hips, grinning with excitement. 'Isn't it great?'

'I don't know,' said Mum, 'because you haven't answered my question yet. What is it?'

'Have a guess,' Dad prompted.

Mum rolled her eyes and sighed. 'It's a box, Ron,' she said flatly. Dad's grin began to fade.

'Of course it's a box. Anyone can see it's a box, but what do you think it does?'

'It makes me cross,' Mum shot back. 'That's what it does.'

Dad's grin vanished. 'What do you mean? How can a box make you cross, for heaven's sake?'

'Because I don't know what it does, Ron, and I want you to tell me and stop asking me to guess when I haven't the faintest clue and if you don't tell me very, VERY soon I shall run away from home and join a circus. Anything for a quiet life.'

Dad looked at me helplessly. Mum wasn't going to play along with his little game so now he wanted me to have a go instead.

'Nicholas? What do you reckon?'

I shrugged. 'Think I'll join Mum at the circus.'

Dad turned to the twins, Cheese and Tomato. If you are wondering why my four-year-old brother and sister are called Cheese and Tomato it's because they were born in the back of a pizza delivery van.

They were! Our car broke down on the way to hospital and Mum climbed in the back of the pizza van. By the time she finally reached the hospital the twins had already been born. Their real names are James and Rebecca, but Dad thought it would be fun to call them Cheese and Tomato and the names have stuck.

Now Dad wanted the twins to guess what the box was. Cheese pulled the plug-in tail.

'Elephant,' he said, and Tomato jumped up and down with laughter. I could tell from her face that she was trying to think of something as silly as possible so as to outdo her brother.

'Sausage-car-bird!' she yelled, pulling her brother on to the floor, where they rolled about in hysterics, repeating their nonsense in as many ways as they could think of. 'Elephant-sausage!'

'Sock-bird-banana!'

At least that was an interesting change but Dad was not amused.

'Sometimes I wonder why I bother with you

lot. What's wrong with this family?'

'Their father, probably,' smiled Mum, smoothing Dad's hair with one hand, as if he were a small child. 'Tell us what it is, Ron,' she suggested. 'Then we can all get on with our lives.'

'You're no fun at all, any of you,' grumbled Dad. 'OK, it's an incubator.'

Now my nose really did wrinkle. 'A what-a-bator?'

'In-cu-ba-tor.'

'But what does it *do*, Dad?'

'Ah,' he began, and his excited grin came bouncing back. 'That's my brilliant idea, you see.

It's for chickens. It's a bit like a sunbed.'

'Since when have chickens needed a sunbed?' asked Mum. 'Do they want a suntan? Most of them are brown already. You'll have them strutting about the garden in dark glasses next.'

'I said it was LIKE a sunbed!' yelled Dad. 'And you don't put *chickens* in there, you dopey doodle, it's for their eggs.'

'Eggs need a suntan?' Mum asked, winding up Dad even more.

'NO! OF COURSE NOT! The box keeps the eggs warm until little fluffy yellow chicks hatch out, going cheep cheepy-cheep, and guess what? We shall have more egg-laying hens. Plus, it will be Easter in a few weeks and lots of people will see the chicks and they'll probably want some for themselves and I can sell off the ones we don't want. Now, am I brilliant or what?'

Mum was desperately pressing her lips together to stop herself bursting into giggles. 'I think you're probably more *what?* than brilliant.'

'Thank you for your support,' growled Dad. 'Huh, I go to all this trouble and you just make fun of me.'

Mum slipped an arm through Dad's. 'There, there. We all love you really,' she smiled. Dad grunted.

I guess I should explain that our back garden is like a mini-farm. We grow lots of vegetables and we now have eight chickens. The first five we got were the cockerel – he's called Captain Birdseye – and four hens, Mavis Moppet, Beaky, Leaky and Poop. Last month we got three new hens, Big Betty, Fusspot and Duvet (who is obviously VERY fluffy), but Poop has always been Cheese's favourite. Tomato loves her too because Poop likes to follow them everywhere.

'Inky-tater,' said Cheese. 'Poop can get a suntan.'

'No,' said Dad. 'You cannot put your pet chicken in here, Tomato. It's for eggs. And it's an incubator, not an inky potato.'

'Can Poop have sunglasses, Daddy?' Tomato pleaded. (She's got some big red ones that she loves.)

Dad groaned and eyed Mum. 'See what you've started?'

Mum smiled back at him. 'Well? Can Tomato's chicken have sunglasses?'

Dad stuck his fingers in his ears and started to sing. 'La-la-la, I can't hear anyone. La-la-la, you're all talking nonsense.'

La-la-la

I took the lid off the box and peered inside. A plastic foam lining covered several rows of heating elements. The lining had lots of egg-shaped hollows in it, enough for thirty eggs.

'Not all the eggs will hatch,' Dad explained. 'But we should have a pretty good success rate. I thought we could take the chicks down to the Easter Fair at your school, Nicholas. Children will love holding them and we can raise money for the new library.'

'Cool,' I said. 'I'll tell Mrs Morgan in class on Monday.'

'Now you're beginning to talk sense,' Mum admitted.

'I always talk sense,' said Dad. 'And don't raise your eyebrows at me like that and you can stop laughing. You too, Nicholas. I expect some support from my eldest son.' Then he strode off in a huff.

He won't be grumpy for long. My dad's not like that. He's always cracking jokes and being daft. He's a bit embarrassing at times but he's great!

Ask Jeremy

Of all the books you have written, which one is your favourite?

I loved writing both **KRAZY KOW SAVES THE WORLD – WELL, ALMOST** and **STUFF**, my first book for teenagers. Both these made me laugh out loud while I was writing and I was pleased with the overall result in each case. I also love writing the stories about Nicholas and his daft family – **MY DAD, MY MUM, MY BROTHER** and so on.

If you couldn't be a writer what would you be?

Well, I'd be pretty fed up for a start, because writing was the one thing I knew I wanted to do from the age of nine onward. But if I DID have to do something else, I would love to be either an accomplished pianist or an artist of some sort. Music and art have played a big part in my whole life and I would love to be involved in them in some way.

What's the best thing about writing stories?

Oh dear – so many things to say here! Getting paid for making things up is pretty high on the list! It's also something you do on your own, inside your own head – nobody can interfere with that. The only boss you have is yourself. And you are creating something that nobody else has made before you. I also love making my readers laugh and want to read more and more.

Did you ever have a nightmare teacher?
(And who was your best ever?)

My nightmare at primary school was Mrs Chappell, long since dead. I knew her secret – she was not actually human. She was a Tyrannosaurus rex in disguise. She taught me for two years when I was in Y5 and Y6, and we didn't like each other at all. My best ever was when I was in Y3 and Y4. Her name was Miss Cox, and she was the one who first encouraged me to write stories. She was brilliant. Sadly, she is long dead too.

When you were a kid you used to play kiss-chase. Did you always do the chasing or did anyone ever chase you?!

I usually did the chasing, but when I got chased, I didn't bother to run very fast! Maybe I shouldn't admit to that! We didn't play kiss-chase at school – it was usually played during holidays. If we had tried playing it at school we would have been in serious trouble. Mind you, I seemed to spend most of my time in trouble of one sort or another, so maybe it wouldn't have mattered that much.

Log on and laugh for hours!

Brand-new 100-mile-an-hour amusement at the KRAZY KLUB.

CRAVING MORE SILLINESS?
Join Jeremy's
KRAZY KLUB
at jeremystrong.co.uk

With hilarious new features:
- Prove how KRAZY you are!
- Addictive games!
- Streaker's blog!

Plus:
Fab Competitions • Fun Stuff • Sneaky Previews
Interactive Polls • Hot Gossip

and lots more rib-tickling treats!

Psssssssssssst!

If you love Puffin Books you should choose

Est. 2008

Puffin Post

Here's what's in it for you:

⭐ 6 magazines

⭐ 6 free books a year (of your choice)

⭐ The chance to see YOUR writing in print

PLUS

⭐ Exclusive author features

⭐ Articles

⭐ Quizzes

⭐ Competitions and games

And that's not all.

You get PRESENTS too.

Simply subscribe here to become a member
puffinpost.co.uk
and wait for your copy to decorate your doorstep.

(WARNING – reading *Puffin Post* may make you late for school.)

It all started with a Scarecrow.

Puffin is seventy years old.
Sounds ancient, doesn't it? But Puffin has never been
so lively. We're always on the lookout for the next big
idea, which is how it began all those years ago.

Penguin Books was a big idea from the mind of
a man called Allen Lane, who in 1935 invented
the quality paperback and changed the world.
**And from great Penguins, great Puffins grew,
changing the face of children's books forever.**

The first four Puffin Picture Books were hatched in 1940 and the
first Puffin story book featured a man with broomstick arms called
Worzel Gummidge. In 1967 Kaye Webb, Puffin Editor, started the
Puffin Club, promising to **'make children into readers'**.
She kept that promise and over 200,000 children became
devoted Puffineers through their quarterly instalments of
Puffin Post, which is now back for a new generation.

Many years from now, we hope you'll look back and
remember Puffin with a smile. **No matter what your age
or what you're into, there's a Puffin for everyone.**
The possibilities are endless, but one thing is for sure:
whether it's a picture book or a paperback, a sticker book
or a hardback, **if it's got that little Puffin
on it – it's bound to be good.**